WHAT EVERY YOUNG RABBIT SHOULD KNOW

BY CAROL DENISON
WITH PICTURES BY KURT WIESE

WHAT EVERY YOUNG RABBIT SHOULD KNOW

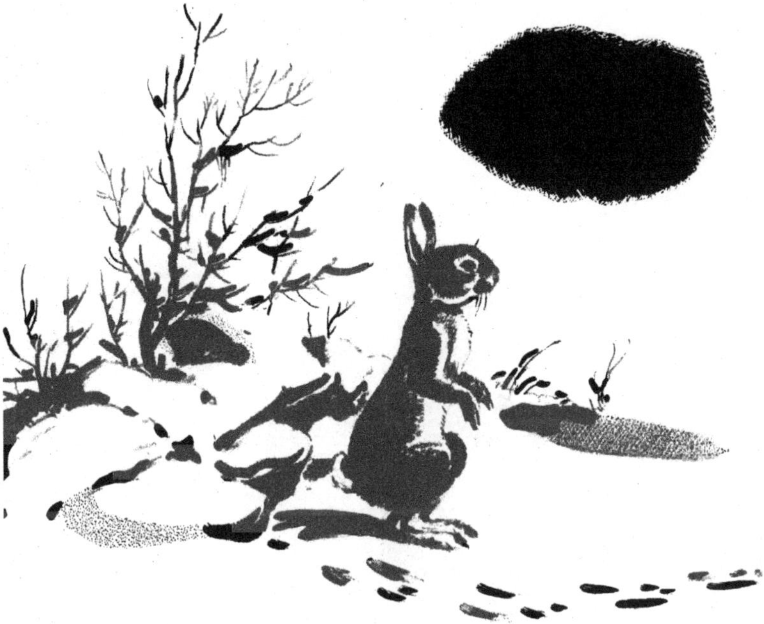

ZING! A *whish-sistle* sounded in the branches of the tree, high above Mrs. Bunny Rabbit Puff-Tail's head.

What was that?

Mrs. Puff-Tail put back her ears, stretched out her long strong hind legs and jumped lickety-split away from there, without waiting to find out.

PING! There was another *whish-sistle* in the twigs of a low bush where Mr. B.R.Puff-Tail was sunning himself.

What was that?

Mr. B.R.Puff-Tail put back his ears, stretched out his long, strong hind legs and jumped lippity-lop after Mrs. Puff-Tail without waiting to find out either.

They both headed for their home, safe in a hollow place surrounded by bramblebushes in the Big Woods.

Mr. and Mrs. Puff-Tail reached the five young rabbits, who were their children, in no time at all because they were such long, strong jumpers. But, my, were they scared!

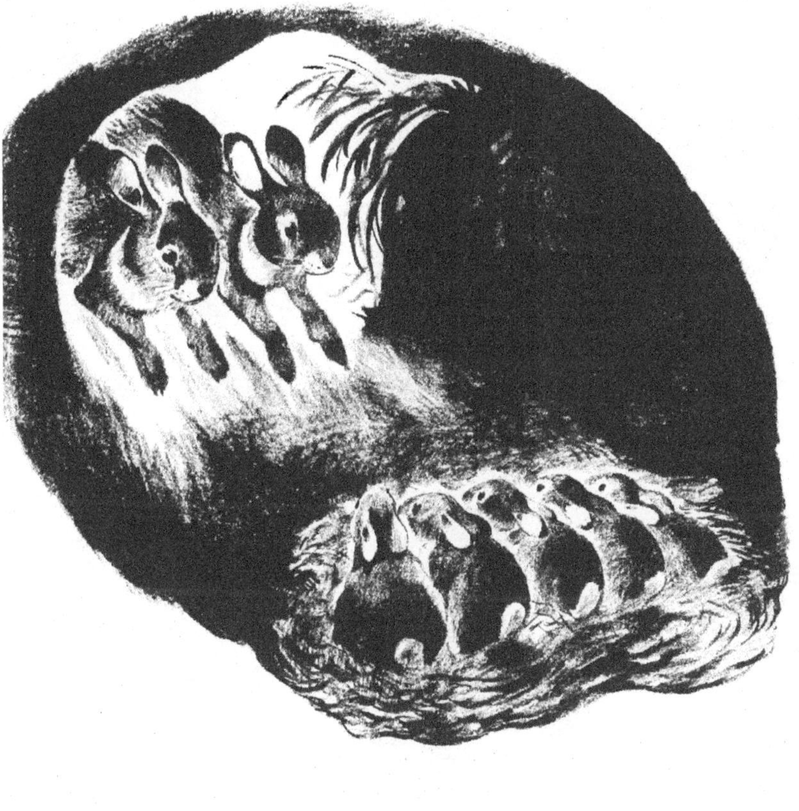

"The hunting days are here again," sighed Mrs. Puff-Tail, as soon as she had caught her breath.

"Soon it will be wintertime," added Mr. Puff-Tail, rubbing his whiskers against his wife's, to comfort her.

"It's time we taught our children another thing or two."

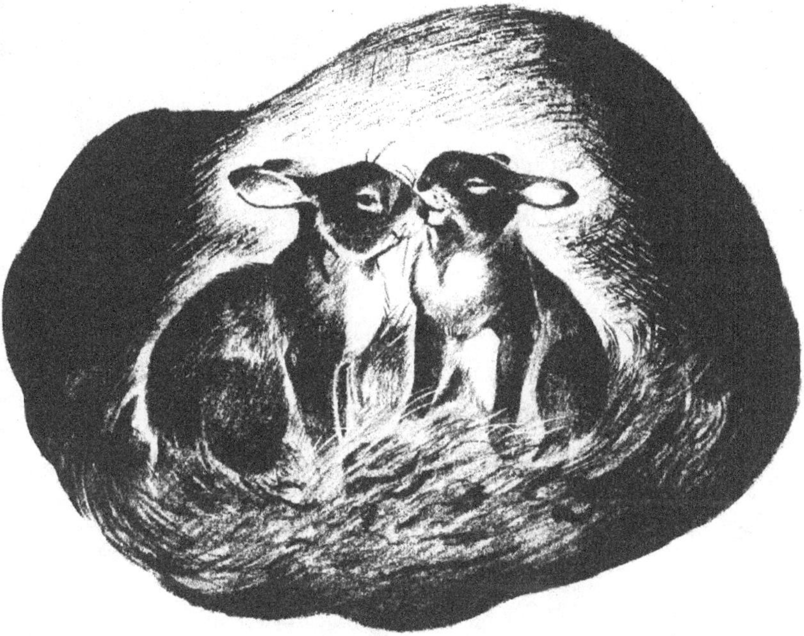

The Mother Rabbit and the Father Rabbit sniffed to one side of them. They sniffed to the other side of them. They stood up on their long, strong hind legs and sniffed straight in front of them.

"Hm! Snow!" They both exclaimed together.

All around them there seemed to be no motion, no sound. But a rabbit could hear a leaf drop. And when a twig snapped, it made a noise like the clap of thunder. The sky was the color of a gray squirrel's fur. The rabbits could tell by the color of the sky and the silence all around that winter must be on its way.

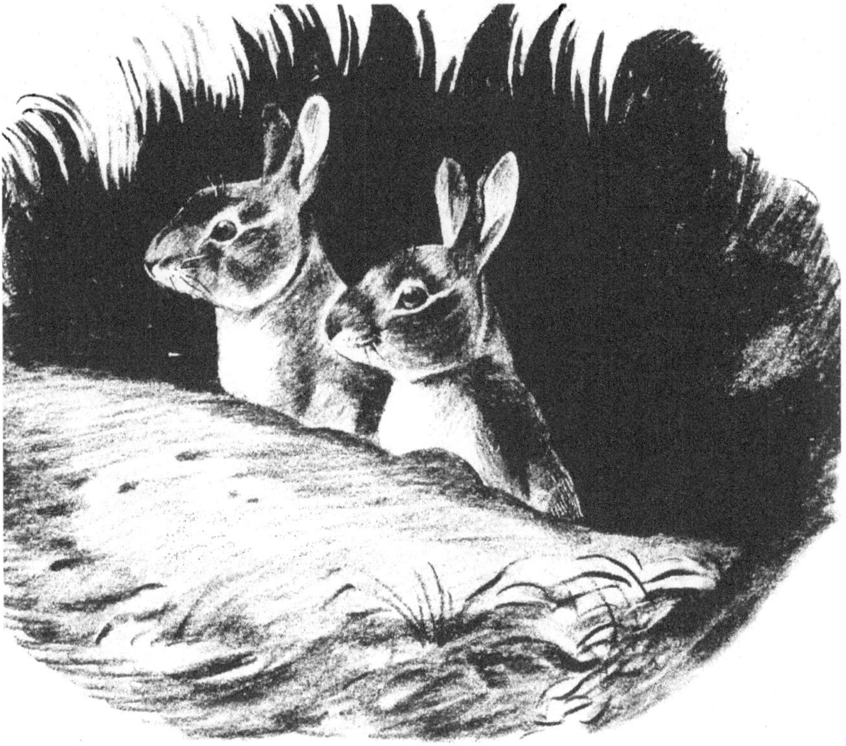

"All we can do is wait for the snow to fall," murmured Mrs. Puff-Tail.

She folded her front paws under her and sank down, ready to sleep beside the children.

Mr. Puff-Tail agreed. Then he, too, folded his front paws under him and sank down beside her.

Soon, the whole Puff-Tail family was fast asleep.

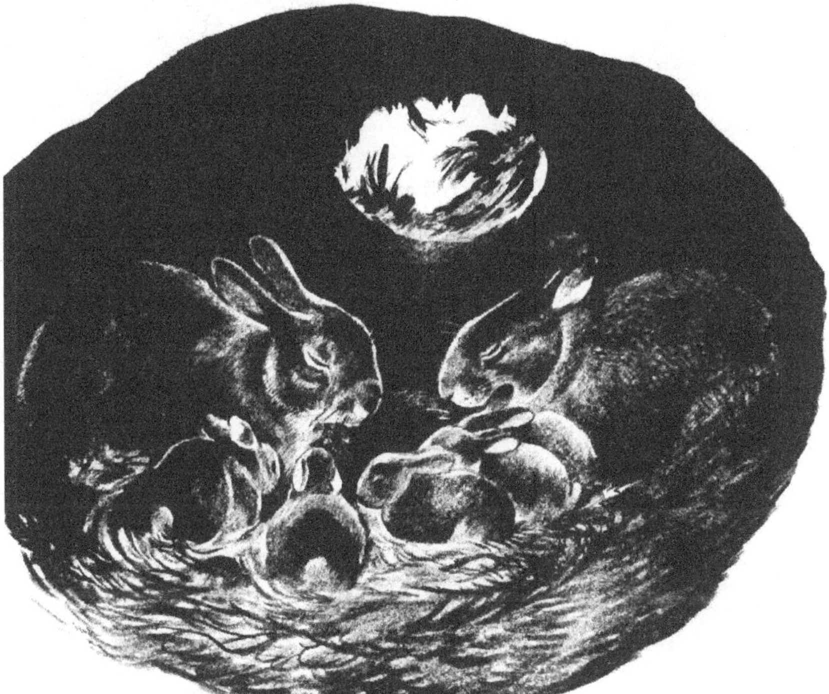

When the sun came up the next morning, Mr. Puff-Tail opened his eyes. Mrs. Puff-Tail opened her eyes. Finally, the five young rabbits popped open their eyes. My, weren't they surprised at what they saw!

"Why, it's whiter than Mummy's teeth!" squeaked one little rabbit.

"Whiter than Daddy's tail!" cried another.

"Than daisies!" piped a third.

"The clouds have fallen down all around us!" said the fourth.

"Oh my! Oh my! Oh my!" was all there was left for the fifth to say.

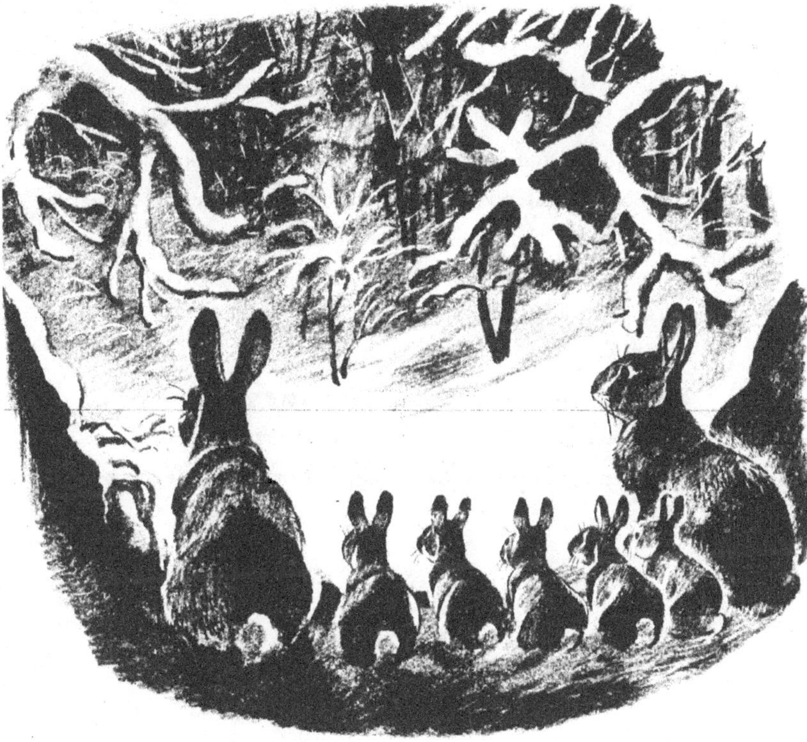

The air smelt like the first bite out of a crisp, cold apple. The air felt like a bath in a cold, rushing brook. Everything was new and exciting to the young rabbits, who had never seen snow before.

The young rabbits twitched their small noses very fast. The young rabbits leaped out from under their cover.

But, quickly, their mother put her feet down on two of them. Their father put his feet down on three of them.

"Wait!" both parents cried together.

"You ought to know a thing or two before you go off in the snow by yourselves!" Their father spoke most sternly to them.

"Believe us, it's for your own good," murmured their mother gently.

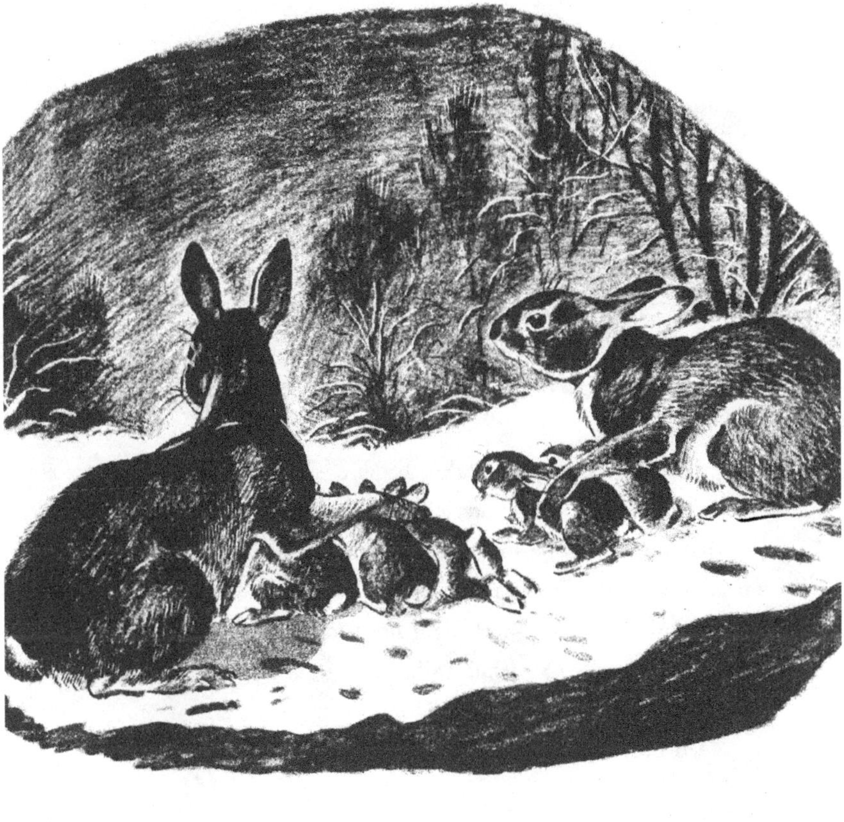

"Form Fives!" cried Father Rabbit.

"Your father wants you to line up in a straight row behind us so that you can all be sure to see," went on Mother Rabbit, who usually took time to explain.

"Now, we'll take short, light hops forward and see what we shall see," directed Mr. Puff-Tail. "No one is to get ahead of me or of your mother, remember."

Off they started, taking short, light hops through the woods.

First, Father Rabbit, then Mother Rabbit, then all five little rabbits in a row behind.

The sun shone through the trees, making black and white designs on the snow around them. Far above, the sky was as blue as a blue bathrobe. The wind was tweaking the branches. Every now and again a branch creaked, a twig cracked.

The young rabbits pricked up their ears, twitched their noses, and turned their heads from side to side so as not to miss anything.

The first thing they hopped up to looked like this—

᠄ ᠄   — ᠄ ᠄   — ᠄ ᠄   — ᠄ ᠄

"Stop!" commanded Father Rabbit. "What's that!"

"We don't know," squeaked the young rabbits in a chorus.

"You should, nothing to be afraid of, though, just the tracks of a—"

"Wait a minute, please, dear," said Mrs. Puff-Tail, gently but firmly. "Let the children guess for themselves."

"Good idea. I'll give them just one hint. It has large ears, but is very small, smaller than you were when you were still just babies. It has pale gray fur on its back and is nearly white on its stomach."

"Don't forget to mention its little pinkish-white feet," Mrs. Puff-Tail reminded him.

"Yes, yes. And it has a tail as skinny as a blade of grass. You can see the mark the tail leaves in the snow between the tracks of its feet."

"I think—I think I know what it is, Father!" The largest rabbit nearly wiggled his nose off, he was so anxious to tell. "I think its a white-footed deer-mouse."

Mr. Puff-Tail thumped his hind foot on the ground, a way rabbits have of showing they are excited about something.

All he said was, "Very good, my boy."

"Freeze still a moment, everybody. Here comes a deer-mouse now. We mustn't frighten him; he's so small."

When Mrs. Puff-Tail said this, all the rabbits stood stock-still, not moving a muscle, not even a whisker. Their father had taught them to freeze still this way when they were very young indeed.

He said it was their best means of protection. They were so quiet now that the little mouse scampered by without ever knowing a single solitary rabbit was near.

Then they all started off again.

"Keep formation!" ordered Father Rabbit.

"Stay in line, dears, that's what your father means. Stay just as you were before," explained their mother.

"Sh! Everybody freeze!" Father Rabbit whispered suddenly.

There was a red flash through the woods. The young rabbits caught the shape of a black shadow on the snow.
That was all.
It was gone.
Their mother seemed unusually upset.
"Look!"—

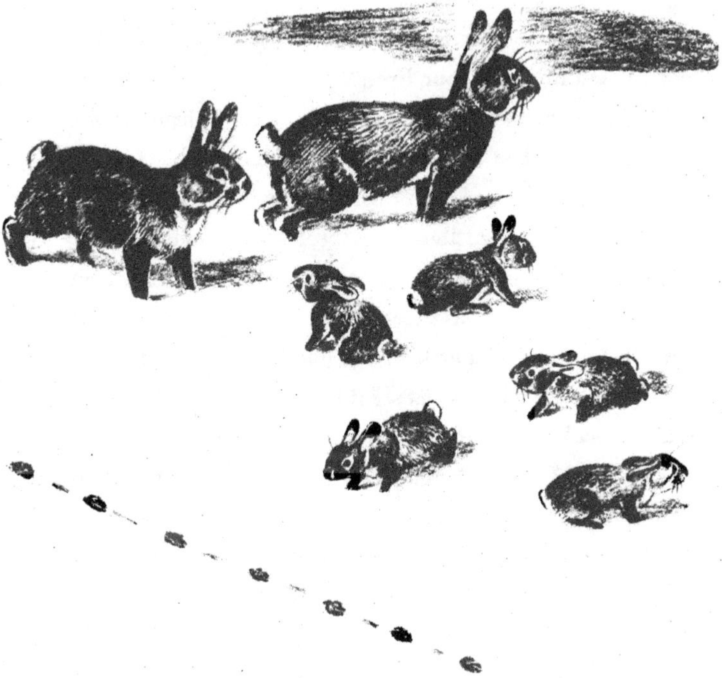

"You must remember those tracks, if you don't remember another blessed thing all your lives!"

"But whose tracks are they! We didn't have a chance to see a thing, did we?" The fifth little rabbit thumped his foot in excitement, just as he had seen his father do.

"Those, my children, those are the tracks of one of your greatest enemies, Bushy the Fox. Look closely. Memorize them well. Notice the print of three feet in line, one ahead of the other. See how the fourth is off a little to one side. That is for balance. Now, everyone close his eyes and see if he can picture exactly how those tracks look—then jump!"

"But where, Daddy, where?" cried the fifth little rabbit, still rather confused.

"It doesn't matter, so long as the Fox can't catch you!"

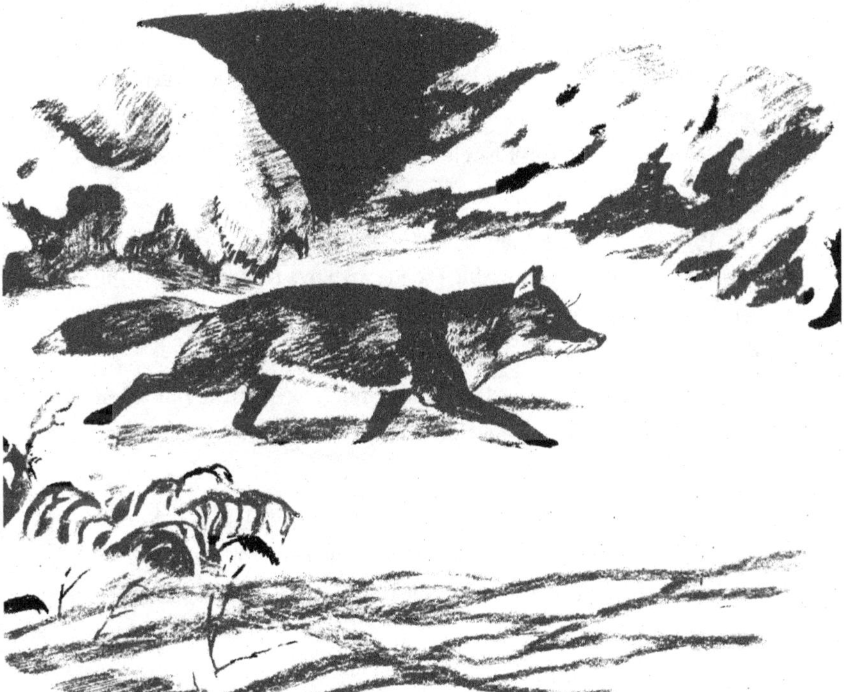

Just then, with a chuck-chuck and chatter, scritch-scratch and screels, someone scolded the Puff-Tail family from a tree high over their heads. All the rabbits looked up.

Two bright eyes were looking down at them. A bushy red-brown tail flicked first to one side of the tree, then to the other.

"He, he!" A fox can't catch me!" chattered a Red Squirrel. "See my tracks? Down there at the bottom of the tree!"

The rabbits took a good look. They saw the tracks of four small feet. There were two big tracks, with five toe-marks showing on each of them. When the rabbits looked up at the squirrel again, they discovered the big tracks belonged to his hind feet.

"I scurry back and forth on the ground, having fun, but when I want to be safe, I climb a tree with my tough hind legs. Want to see me do it?"

The squirrel spread his legs wide around the tree trunk, dug in with his sharp claws and pushed himself hard and fast, up and up. From the very tiptop of the tree they heard him still chattering at them.

"Don't you wish you were made like me!" With a series of big jumps from branch to branch, he rustled off out of sight through the woods.

"My, what a nice way to travel," sighed Mrs. Puff-Tail as she looked down at her own forepaws.

"Good enough for a squirrel, anyway," muttered Mr. Puff-Tail. "Come on, now! We'll cross the brook to the farm and see what we can see."

When they hopped out of the woods, the snow glistened so in the bright sunlight that, at first, the young rabbits could hardly see their parents leaping just ahead of them. Everything sparkled so brightly they could hardly see some new tracks right in front of their twitching little noses.

"Ahem!" said their father, "I think perhaps you're missing something."

"Where? Where?" The young rabbits looked to one side of them. They looked to the other side of them. They looked straight in front of their whiskers. At the very edge of the brook, they saw tracks like these—

"What funny paws that animal must have!" thought the middle-sized rabbit out loud.

"Those aren't paws, those are hoofs!" answered her big brother with scorn.

"How clever of you to know that!" his mother murmured proudly.

"He must have come down to the brook for a drink." Mr. Puff-Tail quivered his whiskers as he thought this out.

"But whose tracks are they?" cried his children.

"Those belong to a deer. If we freeze still over under those bushes, we may see his antlers when he bends down to drink."

The B.R.Puff-Tail family froze still for what seemed like a very long time to the children. Mrs. B.R. even took a little rabbit-nap in the sun while she waited. But there didn't seem to be one single thirsty deer anywhere around that morning.

The young rabbits finally decided there was no use waiting any longer. They had just started off after their parents, who were headed for the farm, when, suddenly, what do you think they saw?

Just as they bounded around the corner of a bush, right straight in front of them, there was a deer! The five young rabbits froze and stared, only their noses quivered with excitement as they gazed up at the deer's huge antlers. The deer stood as still as stone, looking far off over their heads; then, quick as magic, he was off out of sight. The rabbits never knew whether or not he had seen them at all.

They could barely wait to tell their parents of their adventure!

Off up the hill they bounced, white tails bobbing behind them. When they reached the top, they looked down. My, weren't they surprised at what they saw!

A whole hill-full of the queerest marks!

Going one way, they looked like two wide animal tails traveling close together.

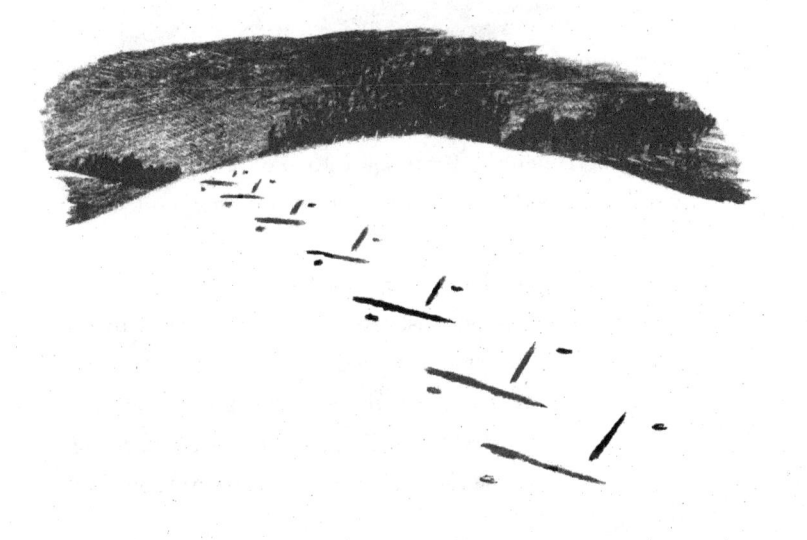

Going the other way, they looked, well, they looked like this—

"Hmmm! Hmmm!" Garrumped Mr. Puff-Tail, who didn't want to admit he really had no idea what animal had made such strange marks in the snow.

There was not another single animal in sight.

Swish! Something flew past the rabbit family's front paws. Something shone on the snow. Something else shone in the air. The rabbits saw only a shadow fly past. Even Mr. Puff-Tail scarcely had time to realize it was Dick, the farmer's son, flying down the hill on shiny new skis, holding his bright metal poles out behind him.

"Whew!" Mr. Puff-Tail wiped one paw across his eyes. "What will People invent next, I want to know!"

As Mrs. Puff-Tail had no way of knowing, she didn't bother to answer her husband. Instead, she started counting noses to be sure that all the children were there.

"Now, then, hop to it, children; on the double!"

As Father Rabbit gave this order, he took an extra-special long leap, to give the young rabbits the right idea, and landed on the edge of a bank above the road.

Out of nowhere, it seemed, came a clatter and a rattle and a clink-clank-clink right below them.

"Jump back!" cried Mrs. Puff-Tail.

"Freeze!" cried Mr. Puff-Tail.

All the little rabbits jumped flip-flop with their backs to the road. Then they froze as stiff as rocks, right where they landed.

The clatter and the rattle and the clink-clank-clink went by below them. But not one rabbit saw what it was. They had their eyes tightly closed, they were so scared.

When they opened their eyes again, suddenly, or so it seemed, everything was still again.

After such a horrible racket, the whole outdoors was quieter than ever before.

Mr. Puff-Tail waited until his nose stopped wabbling with fright. When he was sure there was no more danger, he scurried off to see what had made such a fearful noise. He bounded back again in no time and began thumping his hind foot.

"Ah! Just as I thought! That's what did it, that's what did it!" Mr. Puff-Tail was so excited that he couldn't go on for a moment.

Mrs. Puff-Tail hopped over and squatted down beside him. "Did what, dear?"

"Made that racket. Made those marks in the road. Tire tracks, that's what they are. Must have been a car that swooshed past us. Dangerous things, cars! Come, let's hop out of here!"

"Shall we take the children through the cow pasture to the garden back of the barn, next?" Mrs. Puff-Tail sounded just a bit worried. "I really think we ought to stop somewhere soon for a bite to eat. It's way past the children's lunch time."

"Yes, yes." Mr. Puff-Tail agreed with his wife. "Not much to learn on the way, anyhow. Cows, horse, chickens, maybe—you children should have no trouble recognizing their tracks in the snow."

"I could recognize a horseshoe mark," exclaimed the largest rabbit.

"I could rec- recognize a cow's track," cried his sister, the middle-sized rabbit.

" 'C'nize chickie!" puffed the smallest rabbit, who was having a little trouble keeping up with the rest now.

With a hop-leap-jump, all the rabbits bounced off in formation over the snow to the pasture.

Sure enough, the largest rabbit found a horseshoe mark on the way. This is how it looked—

This is the mark of the cow's hoof which the middle-sized rabbit pointed out in the pasture—

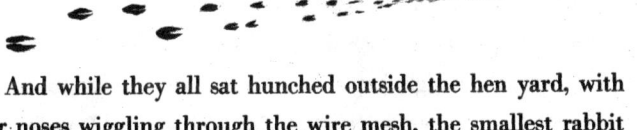

And while they all sat hunched outside the hen yard, with their noses wiggling through the wire mesh, the smallest rabbit showed them he really did know what the tracks a chicken makes look like.

With a hop and a leap and a jump, the Puff-Tail family went on towards the garden in back of the barn.

"Sh!" whispered Father Rabbit. "Freeze! All of you!"

He took a short, light hop ahead of them, stood up on his hind feet, drooped his forelegs in front of him, and wiggled his nose in the air.

Then he plopped down on all fours again. "I just thought I smelt people. It's only their tracks, though. See what I mean?"

The young rabbits hoppd up to where their father was and took a good look.

They saw two great big steps.

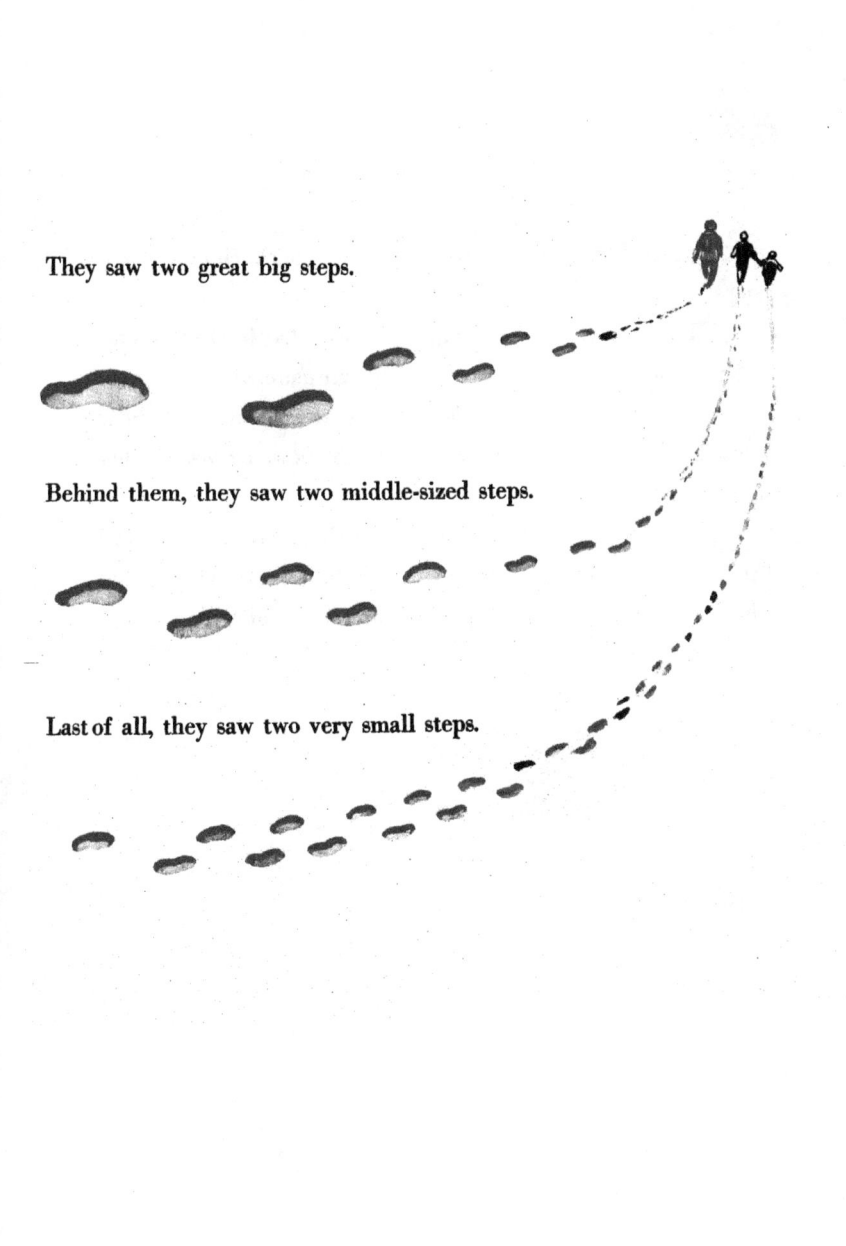

Behind them, they saw two middle-sized steps.

Last of all, they saw two very small steps.

Mother Rabbit murmured to herself, "Such cunning baby steps!"

"Hmph!" said her husband, who wasn't too fond of people. "We haven't got all day to sit around on our haunches, gawping at them! Hurry up, now." Father Rabbit was sometimes a little cantankerous when he was hungry—right now, he was mighty hungry.

In fact, they were all so hungry that they never even noticed the prints of a cat's feet across their path; they never even noticed the cat himself, sunning on a fence-post above them, with both her eyes closed.

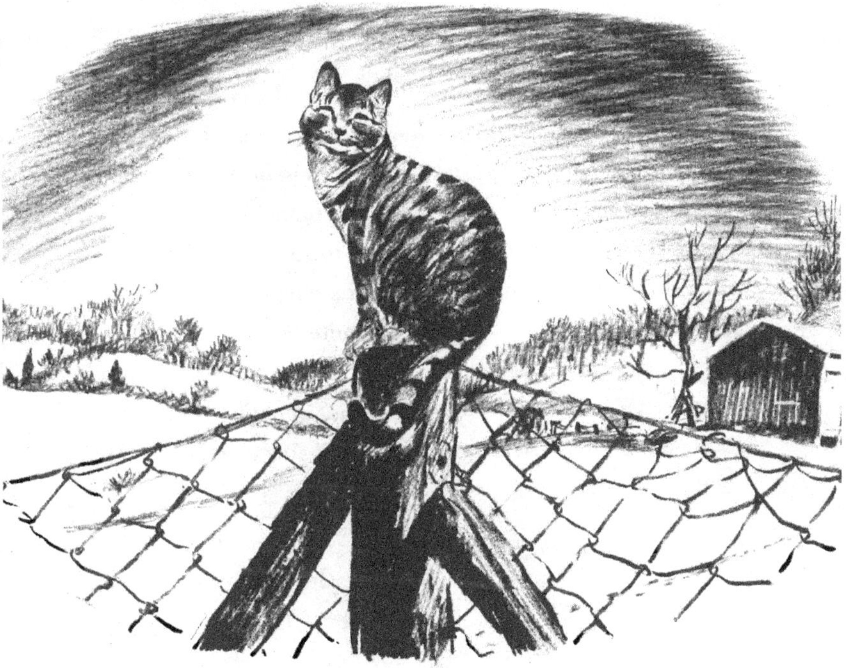

"I smell turnips!" squealed the next to the smallest rabbit, who, up to now, hadn't said a word since they'd started. The next to the smallest rabbit could smell food, even in his sleep.

It didn't take those rabbits more than three hops to get inside that garden, once they smelled those turnips. It didn't take Father Rabbit more than a scrabble and a scrape to dig up frozen turnips, even though the ground was quite hard. And it didn't take any time at all before the Puff-Tail family were gnawing turnips out of the sides of their mouths, wabbling their noses, wiggling their whiskers, and thoroughly enjoying their lunch. My, but they were hungry!

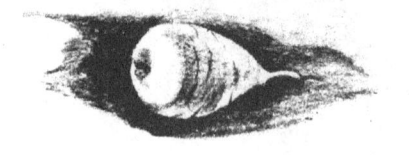

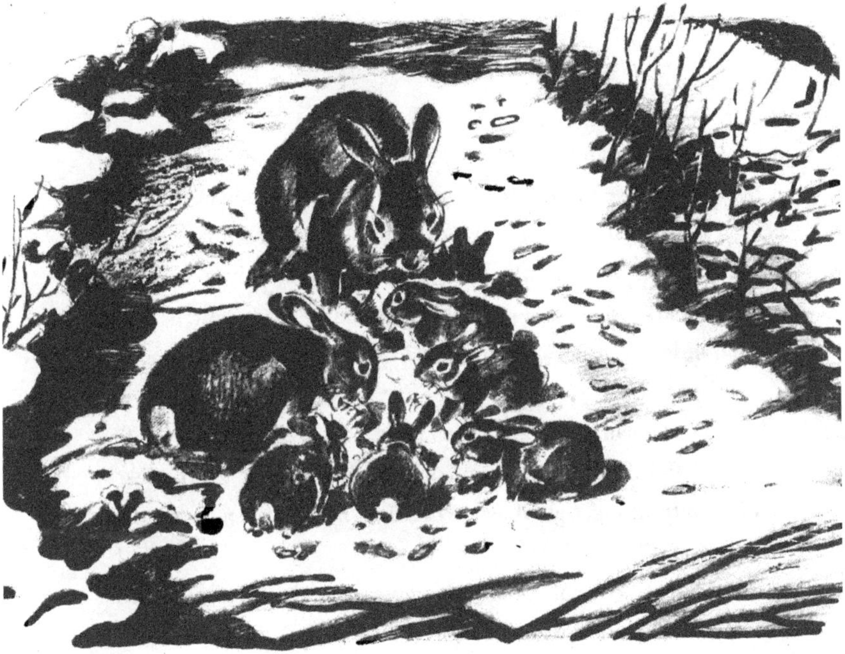

Just as they were beginning to feel a little bit better and a little bit fuller, there was a terrible noise on the other side of the barn.

"Yap! Yap! Yap!" A noisy noise—a frightening noise to the rabbits. How would rabbits know it was only a watchdog taking barking exercises? Watchdogs must keep their barks in good order to protect their masters' property, of course.

"Yap! Yap!"

No one had to tell anyone to freeze stock-still this time. The B.R. Puff-Tail family were so frightened they froze every muscle without thinking, right down to the last whisker-tip on the smallest rabbit of all.

"Yap!" The noise was coming nearer. The noise was getting louder. The noise was coming right AROUND the barn itself.

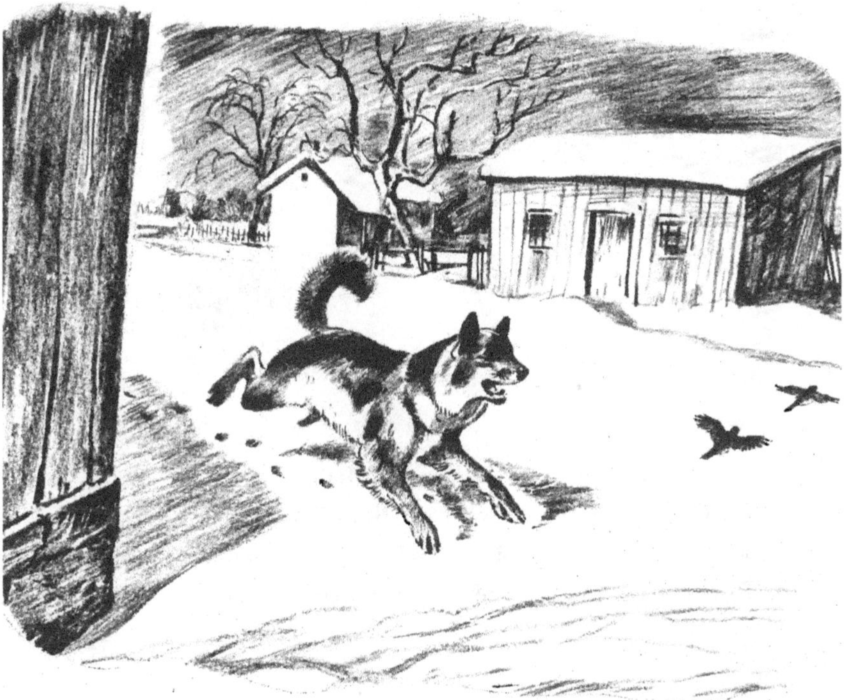

"Run for your lives!" whispered Mother Rabbit.

Every single member of that B.R. Puff-Tail family stretched out his long, strong hind legs and jumped an enormous jump. Then up went their tails and they ran lickety-lop away from there.

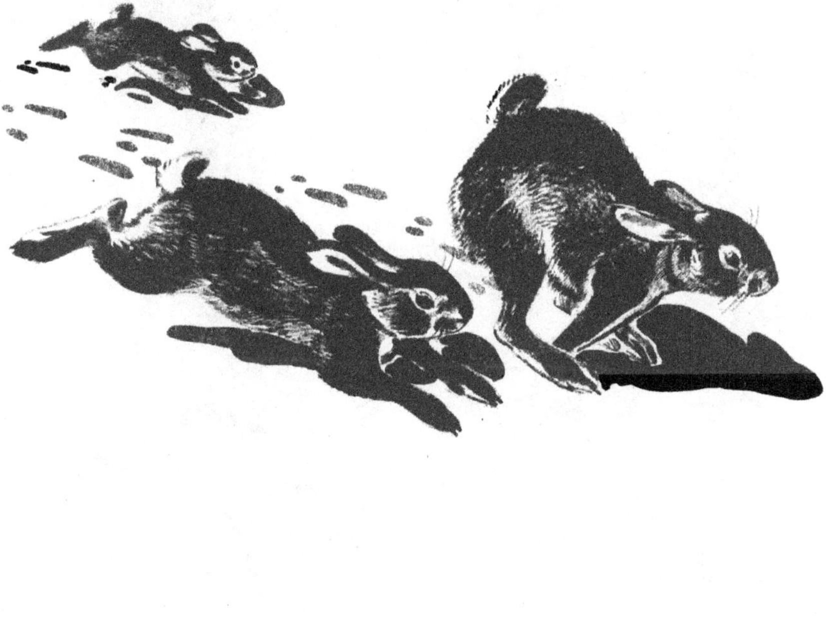

Back around the corner of the barn.

Over the cat prints.

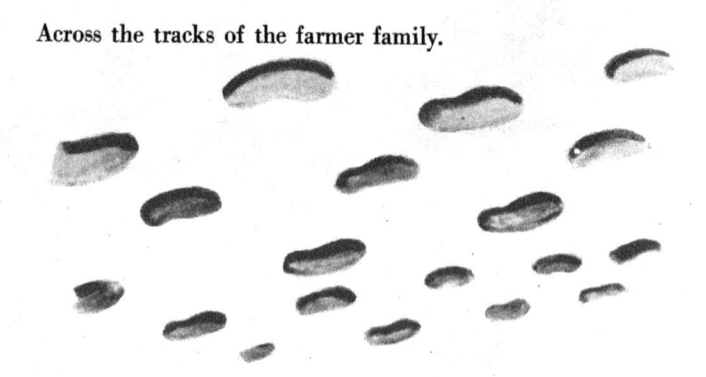

Across the tracks of the farmer family.

Back past the chicken tracks in the hen yard.

Back over the cow tracks.

Around the horseshoe marks.

In between the tire-tracks.

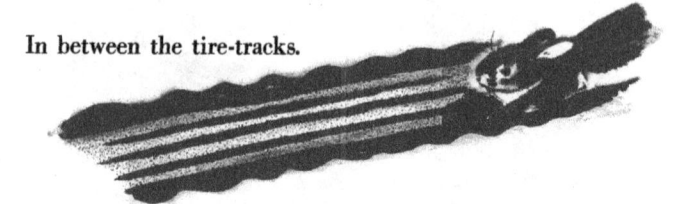

Up over the hill-full of skii tracks.

Down across the brook with the deer marks on its banks.

Around the squirrel's tree.

Lickety-split across the tracks the fox made.

Lippity-lop by the mouse tracks,

then ker-plop!

The Puff-Tail family rolled over the edge of their nest and under the grass and fur coverlet, where they huddled and shivered and shook, huddled and quivered, wobbling their noses with fright.

When Mrs. Puff-Tail got back enough breath, she began to comfort all her children at once by rubbing their whiskers. Or, at least, she tried to.

"That was a very narrow escape!" Mr. Puff-Tail managed to mutter. "Another moment and that dog might—"

"B.R.!" shrieked his wife, who never called her husband by his initials unless there was a Catastrophe or an Extreme Emergency. "B.R.! Where is my baby? Where is Huff, our littlest child?"

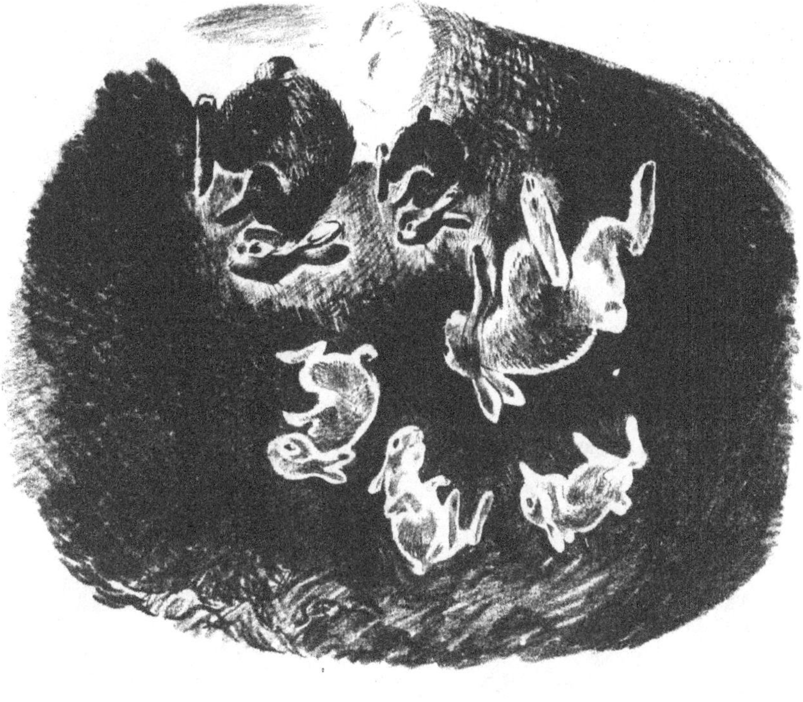

Where indeed was little Huff Puff-Tail?

Mr. Puff-Tail stood up on his hind legs and looked all around the ground near their home. Mrs. Puff-Tail stood on her hind legs and looked all around the nest, too. All the little Puff-Tails who were left stood up and looked, but they couldn't see over the edge.

"You stay here, my dear, and I'll start right out on a searching party," said Mr. Puff-Tail nervously. "I'll run circles around our home and see what I can see."

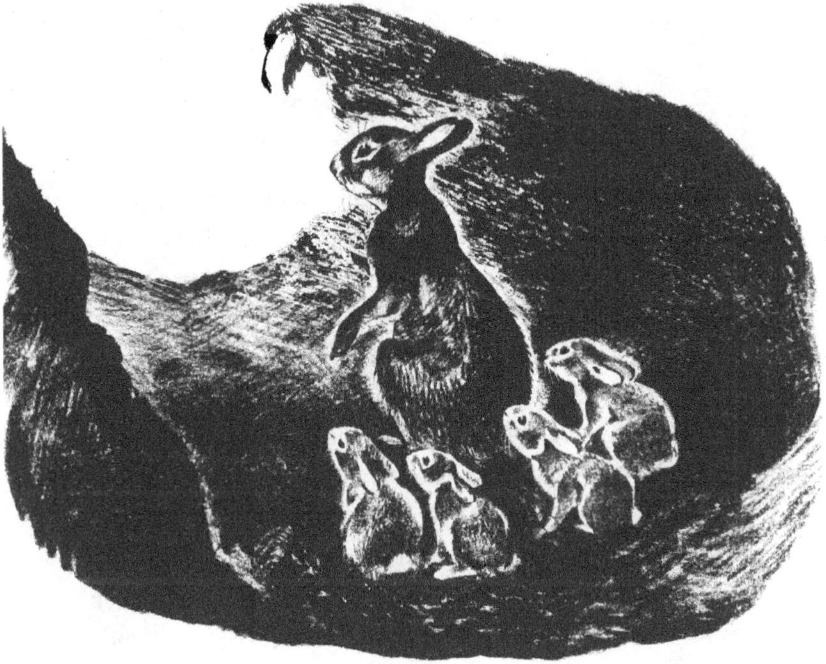

Mrs. Puff-Tail had a hard time keeping his white tail in sight, as it bounced over the snow, because her eyes were so full of tears.

In fact, she was crying so hard that she never even saw a streak with a shadow coming lippity-lop towards her from the other side.

All of a sudden, she felt a soft little plop down next to her.

"Mummy! Mummy! I found some new tracks. Lots and lots and lots of tracks—and I followed them and they came right here, and Mummy, what kind of dangerous animal made those tracks!"

But Mrs. Puff-Tail was so glad to see her baby, Huff Puff-Tail, that she didn't care what kind of an animal had made them. She just wanted to cuddle her baby and rub his whiskers and thump her hind foot all at once. As for Huff, he was pressed so tightly against her, he could hardly wiggle his nose enough to ask her more questions.

Just then, his father circled back in sight.

"He's home, dear; he's safe," cried Mrs. Puff-Tail to her husband.

In between his mother's whisker-rubbings, Huff Puff-Tail managed to tell his father about his adventures.

"Daddy, I found some new tracks and they came right here and I followed them all by myself and I think there must be a dangerous animal right outside somewhere! Look, Daddy, please look!"

Once more, his father stood up on his long, strong hind legs and looked all around.

Then he laughed. And he laughed and he laughed and he just couldn't stop laughing.

"Those are—ha! ha! Those are—ho! ho! Silly boy, those are OUR tracks! Your tracks and your mother's and your brothers' and your sisters'! *He! He! Ho! Ho! Ha! Ha!*"

Then all the other young rabbits started to laugh and they laughed and they laughed and they couldn't stop laughing.

Little Huff Puff-Tail felt very sad and very silly—very, very silly.

But his mother didn't laugh. She just went on rubbing his whiskers to comfort him.

Printed in the USA
CPSIA information can be obtained
at www.ICGtesting.com
LVHW040058111023
760674LV00003B/15

9 781445 514505